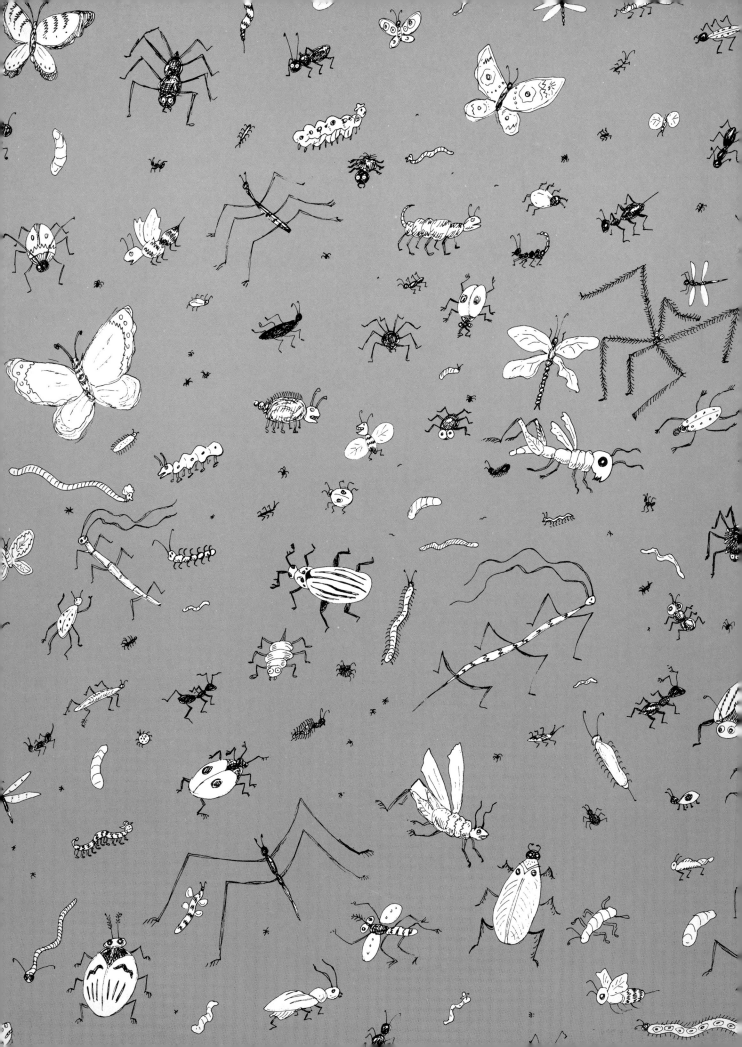

Library of Congress Cataloging-in-Publication Data
Olsen, Alfa–Betty.   Gabby the shrew /
by Alfa–Betty Olsen and Marshall Efron ; illustrated by Roz Chast.   p.   cm.
SUMMARY: A small shrew with a very LARGE voice causes a great deal of trouble
when he sets out with his stomach in search of something to eat.
ISBN 0–679–84499–6 (trade) – ISBN 0–679–94499–0 (lib. bdg.)
[1. Shrews–Fiction.   2. Food habits–Fiction.   3. Noise–Fiction.   4. Humorous stories.]
I. Efron, Marshall.   II. Chast, Roz, ill.   III. Title.   PZ7.05174Gab   1994   [E]–dc20   92–31902

Manufactured in the United States of America   10 9 8 7 6 5 4 3 2 1

GABBY
THE
SHREW

by Alfa-Betty Olsen and Marshall Efron
illustrated by Roz Chast

RANDOM HOUSE 🏠 NEW YORK

A few weeks ago, Gabby, a baby shrew as big as a plum pit, awoke hungry as usual; and his mom, who was as big as a peach pit, served him his usual breakfast–a meal that was bigger than he was.

He ate:

- a couple of crunchy crickets,
- a group of juicy grasshoppers,
- one fresh frog,
- a pair of slippery salamanders,
- several tasty moths,
- a pack of peppery millipedes,
- a squishy centipede,
- a number of succulent beetles,
- a few chewy worms,
- and other assorted creepies, crawlies, and wingies of various flavors.

Gabby finished every bit of his breakfast, but it wasn't enough.

"THANK YOU, MOM. I'D LIKE ANOTHER HELPING," he shouted, because shrews never whisper when they can shout, never shout when they can shriek, and if they can holler, they like it even better. That's the way shrews are.

"YOUR COMMAND IS MY DESIRE.
I'LL GO HUNT SOME MORE SLIMIES,"
screamed Gabby's mom. "SEE YOU LATER."

Gabby and his mom made such a racket that the leaves shivered on the trees, the clouds overhead floated away, the flowers in the neighborhood closed up for the night in the morning, and an owl in the tree above woke up and fainted from the noise. But Gabby and his mom didn't care, because they were shrews.

The moment Gabby's mom left, Gabby's stomach growled.
"**If we go out now,**" it rumbled, "**I bet we find good grub right away.**"
"**DO YOU THINK SO?**" shrieked Gabby, and somewhere a buttercup melted.
"**Definitely,**" whispered his stomach.

"OKAY, LET'S GO," yelled Gabby so loudly that
a forget-me-not forgot everything she had been told
not to forget.

Gabby leaped through the door and ran up the
dirt tunnel . . .

. . . till he was out on the floor of the forest. It was the first time little Gabby had ever left the cozy hole in the ground he called home.

"**WOW!**" screamed Gabby, looking a fern in the face. "**THIS IS NICE.**"

"Uh–oh," said a ladybug, "I hear a shrew coming on."

"Quick, let's go to California," said her children. And they did. So did every other insect for miles around. When Gabby sniffed the air and tried to catch a whiff of something he could eat, the air was empty.

Gabby started walking.

"I'LL EAT ANYTHING THAT'S FOOD," he boomed.

"Me too," said his stomach.

Gabby came to a big black stone dripping with moss and covered with mud.

Gabby crunched a bite out of it and chewed.

"POOH!" he yelled. **"THIS ISN'T FOOD."**
"It's as hard as a rock," growled his stomach.

Gabby walked . . .

and walked . . .

And as he walked, time marched on ahead of him and the afternoon ran out.

"WE'VE BEEN OUT FOR HOURS, AND WE HAVEN'T SEEN ONE CRITTER WE CAN EAT. WHERE DID THEY ALL GO?" shouted Gabby, and the last two lightning bugs left in the forest shorted out and went dark for the duration.

"Don't ask me. I'm down here. I can't see anything," rumbled his stomach.

Gabby climbed a tall, straight pine tree. When he got
to the top, he saw a house at the edge of the forest.

The door of the house opened, and Gabby heard a woman's voice call out, "Billy Torkelsen! Time to eat." **"DID SHE SAY 'TIME TO EAT'?"** boomed Gabby. **"That's what it sounded like to me,"** answered his stomach.

Gabby jumped down from the tree, ran to the house, and walked in under the front door.

He strode into the dining room and smiled, showing his tiny teeth. **"WHAT'S FOR DINNER?"** he screeched in his sweetest ear-piercing voice. Then he rolled onto his back and waved his little feet in the air.

"A mouse with a loudspeaker!" screamed Mrs. Torkelsen.

She covered her ears, ran from the room, and returned with the Torkelsen cat, Sidney. "You're a cat, Sidney," she said. "Cats catch mice. Now go to work."

"He's too small to be a mouse," thought Sidney. "He smells bad, and he's loud. That can mean only one thing: he's a shrew. This house is in trouble."

Sidney ran out of the house and sat on top of the
Torkelsen car.
"I'll be back," he meowed. "I'm just not sure when."

"I'll get this mouse," said Mr. Torkelsen. "Where is it?"

"There." Mrs. Torkelsen pointed.

Mr. Torkelsen looked, but Gabby was gone. He was inside the terrarium eating the head off a plastic dinosaur.

"PEUGHGH!" he bellowed. **"THAT WASN'T FOOD."**

"I liked it, but it was dry," said his stomach.

Then Gabby ate all the curlicues in the rug. **"THOSE WORMS WERE VERY HAIRY,"** he screamed.

"**I didn't like them,**" said his stomach. "**Don't send me any more.**"

"Go get him!" wailed Mrs. Torkelsen, but before Mr. Torkelsen could get going, Gabby had run to the wallpaper and chewed half the butterflies out of the pattern.

"POOH!" howled Gabby. **"THAT WASN'T FOOD EITHER."**

Mr. Torkelsen snuck up behind Gabby with a fly swatter and raised it high in the air. But Gabby didn't notice because he was staring at the tassel on the window shade. **"A BIG FAT SPIDER WITH LONG SILKY LEGS!"** Gabby shouted.

Mr. Torkelsen brought the fly swatter down as hard as he could . . .

. . . just as Gabby jumped onto the tassel and
sank his sharp pointy little teeth into it. The
shade shot up and took Gabby with it.
    The shade unrolled, and Gabby was
dropped down.

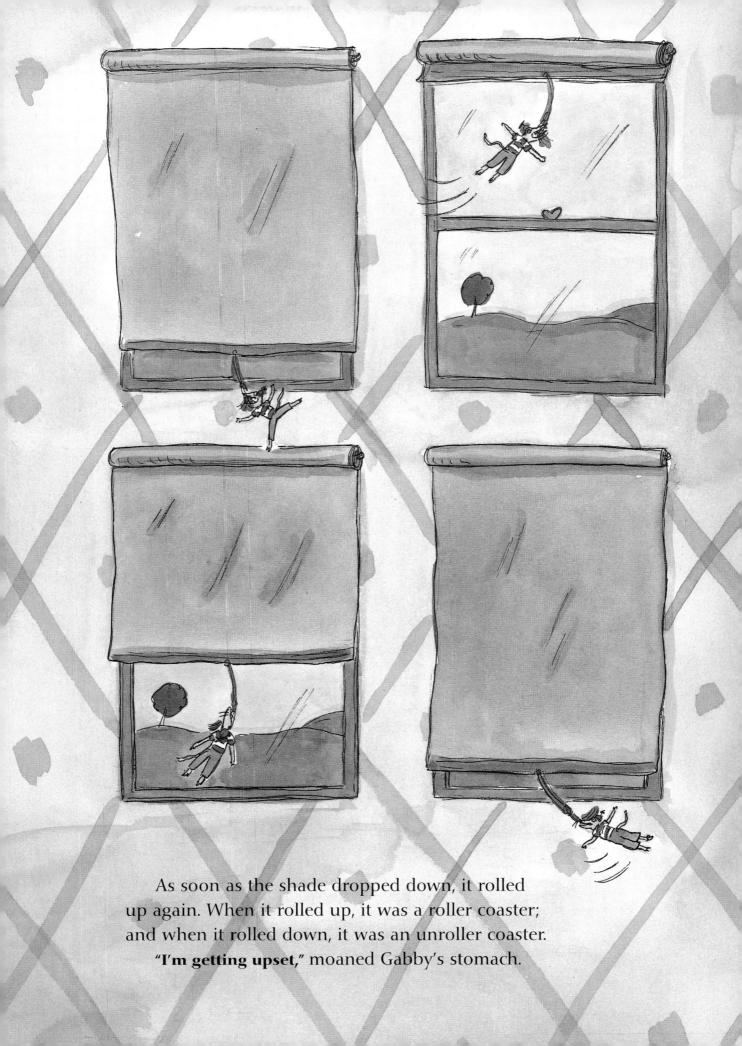

As soon as the shade dropped down, it rolled
up again. When it rolled up, it was a roller coaster;
and when it rolled down, it was an unroller coaster.
"I'm getting upset," moaned Gabby's stomach.

At that very moment Gabby's mom
arrived home with a big bag of bugs.
   "DINNER'S HERE!" she boomed sweetly.
She braced herself for little Gabby's greeting,
but there was none.
   "MY BEAUTIFUL BABY IS GONE!" she
sobbed, and set out to look for Gabby.

Back at the Torkelsen house, the shade shot up and Gabby thundered **"HELP MEEEEEEEE!"** louder than he'd ever thundered before. All the windows in the house shattered, and the stairs fell in with a big cracking thunk.

Deep in the forest, Gabby's mom stopped in her tracks and listened.

"THAT'S MY GABBY," she bellowed, and she began to run.
Gabby's mom reached the Torkelsen house. She saw the porch
detach itself and crumble into dust. Then she noticed the shade
that was rolling up and down.

"MY BABY IS IN THAT HOUSE. I KNOW IT," she shrilled.
"HEELLLPP!" blared Gabby.

The big chandelier in the entrance hall fell from the
ceiling and exploded on the floor with a terrible crash and
the sounds of a thousand tinkles.

Gabby's mom climbed through a broken window.
Her whiskers bristled. Her tiny eyes darted fire. **"GIVE ME
BACK MY SON!"** she raged at the Torkelsens.

"Who's keeping him?" asked Mr. Torkelsen.

"We don't want him," said Mrs. Torkelsen.

"Nobody needs a loud mouse," said Billy.

"HE'S NOT A LOUD MOUSE. HE'S A SHREW!"
Gabby's mom proclaimed proudly.

"WELL, NOBODY NEEDS A LOUD SHREW EITHER,"
shouted the Torkelsens, and the chimney fell in, the
fireplace blew out, and the roof came apart in many places.

**"TAKE YOUR TEETH OUT OF THE TASSEL,
GABBY DARLING,"** screamed Gabby's mom. **"WE'RE
GOING HOME."**

"GOOD–BYE AND GOOD RIDDANCE!" shouted
the Torkelsens, and a wall of their house split open.
"THANK YOU VERY MUCH," screeched Gabby's
mom, and Gabby and his mom walked out through the
jagged crack, crossed the lawn, and entered the forest,
heading for home.

Deep in the woods, where everything alive was fast asleep and everywhere was very dark, Gabby yodeled a loud, jolly song: **"I LOVE A BUG! I LOVE AN INSECT! I LOVE A WORM!"**

"PIPE DOWN!" yelled a mouse, a fox, a rabbit, a turtle, a groundhog, a raccoon, a porcupine, and an entire ant colony.

"I LOVE A SWEET MOTH FOR DESSERT. I LOVE MY MOM! I LOVE MYSELF! I LOVE MY STOMACH! MY STOMACH LOVES ME!" sang Gabby, who didn't care, because he was a shrew.

Every living creature in the forest screamed "GABBY, SHUTTT UPPP!"

"HALLELUJAH, I'M A SHREW!" sang
Gabby in his loudest voice.
Suddenly the moon in the sky overhead
broke with a giant shiver.

Millions of tiny moon bits fell to earth and lit up the forest.
"UH–OH!" yelled Gabby. **"DID I DO SOMETHING BAD?"**

"OF COURSE NOT, DEAR," screamed Gabby's mom.
"WE'LL GET A NEW MOON AT THE END OF THE MONTH—
WE ALWAYS DO."

"IN THAT CASE, I WON'T WORRY," bellowed Gabby.
"LET'S GO HOME."

So Gabby and his mother walked home, had a big snack,
curled up together, and went to sleep.

DATE DUE

APR 1 9 96			
JUN 1 6 01			
DEC 2 0 2004			
JUN 2 6 2006			
GAYLORD			PRINTED IN U.S.A.